The Farmer's Lunch

Written by Paul Shipton
Illustrated by John Gordon

Collins

2

4

6

8

13

A map of the farm

Ideas for guided reading

Learning objectives: use talk to organise, sequence and clarify thinking, ideas, feelings and events; use language to imagine and recreate roles and experiences; read a range of familiar and common words and simple sentences independently; retell narratives in the correct sequence, drawing on the language patterns of stories

Curriculum links: Personal, Social and Emotional Development: Be confident to try new activities, initiate ideas and speak in a familiar group

High frequency words: my

Interest words: farmer, lunch, sandwich, banana, apple, biscuit, camera, birthday, where's

Word count: 18

Resources: whiteboard, speech bubbles

Getting started

- Ask children to tell the group what they like eating for lunch. Make a list of some ideas on a whiteboard.

- Look at the front and back covers together. In pairs, ask children to read the title and the blurb, and to describe what is happening in the pictures.

- Ask children to share their ideas and to predict what is going to happen in the story.

Reading and responding

- Read pp2–3 together. Discuss the function of the question mark. Reread the question, modelling how to use expression.

- Introduce the term *speech bubble*. Explain that the farmer is speaking aloud.

- Remind children of the strategies that they can use to attempt new words like *lunch*, including using the context and pictures.

- Ask children to read the story independently and aloud to the end.